D0055041
A QUICK & EASY GUIDE TO
QUEER & TRANS
IDENTITIES
MADY G & J.R. ZUCKERBERG

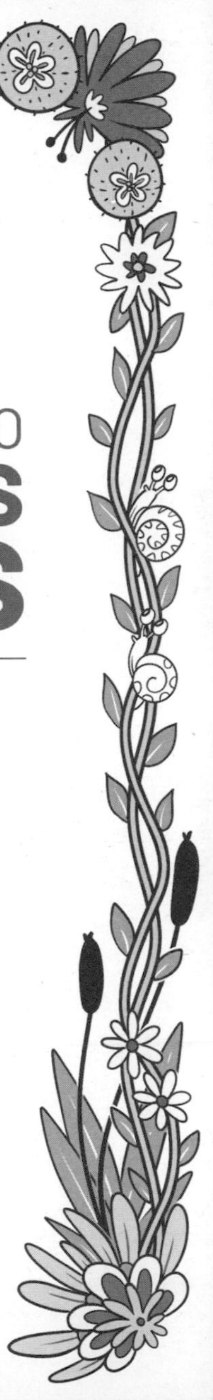

A QUICK & EASY GUIDE TO QUEER & TRANS IDENTITIES

MADY G & J.R. ZUCKERBERG

A LIMERENCE PRESS
PUBLICATION

Designed by Kate Z. Stone
Edited by Ari Yarwood

Published by Limerence Press, Inc.
LIMERENCE PRESS IS AN IMPRINT OF ONI PRESS, INC.
JOE NOZEMACK founder & chief financial officer
JAMES LUCAS JONES publisher
CHARLIE CHU v.p. of creative & business development
BRAD ROOKS director of operations
MELISSA MESZAROS director of publicity
MARGOT WOOD director of sales
SANDY TANAKA marketing design manager
AMBER O'NEILL special projects manager
TROY LOOK director of design & production
KATE Z. STONE senior graphic designer
SONJA SYNAK graphic designer
ANGIE KNOWLES digital prepress lead
ARI YARWOOD executive editor
SARAH GAYDOS editorial director of licensed publishing
ROBIN HERRERA senior editor
DESIREE WILSON associate editor
MICHELLE NGUYEN executive assistant
JUNG LEE logistics coordinator
SCOTT SHARKEY warehouse assistant

LimerencePress.com
Limerencepress.tumblr.com
@Limerencepress

madyg.com / @MadyGComics
jrzuckerberg.com / @helloitsjr

First Edition: April 2019
ISBN: 978-1-62010-586-3
eISBN: 978-1-62010-587-0

Library of Congress Control Number: 2018958550

A Quick & Easy Guide to Queer & Trans Identities, April 2019. Published by Limerence Press, Inc. 1319 SE Martin Luther King Jr. Blvd., Suite 240, Portland, OR 97214.

PRINTED IN CHINA.

10 9 8 7 6 5 4 3 2

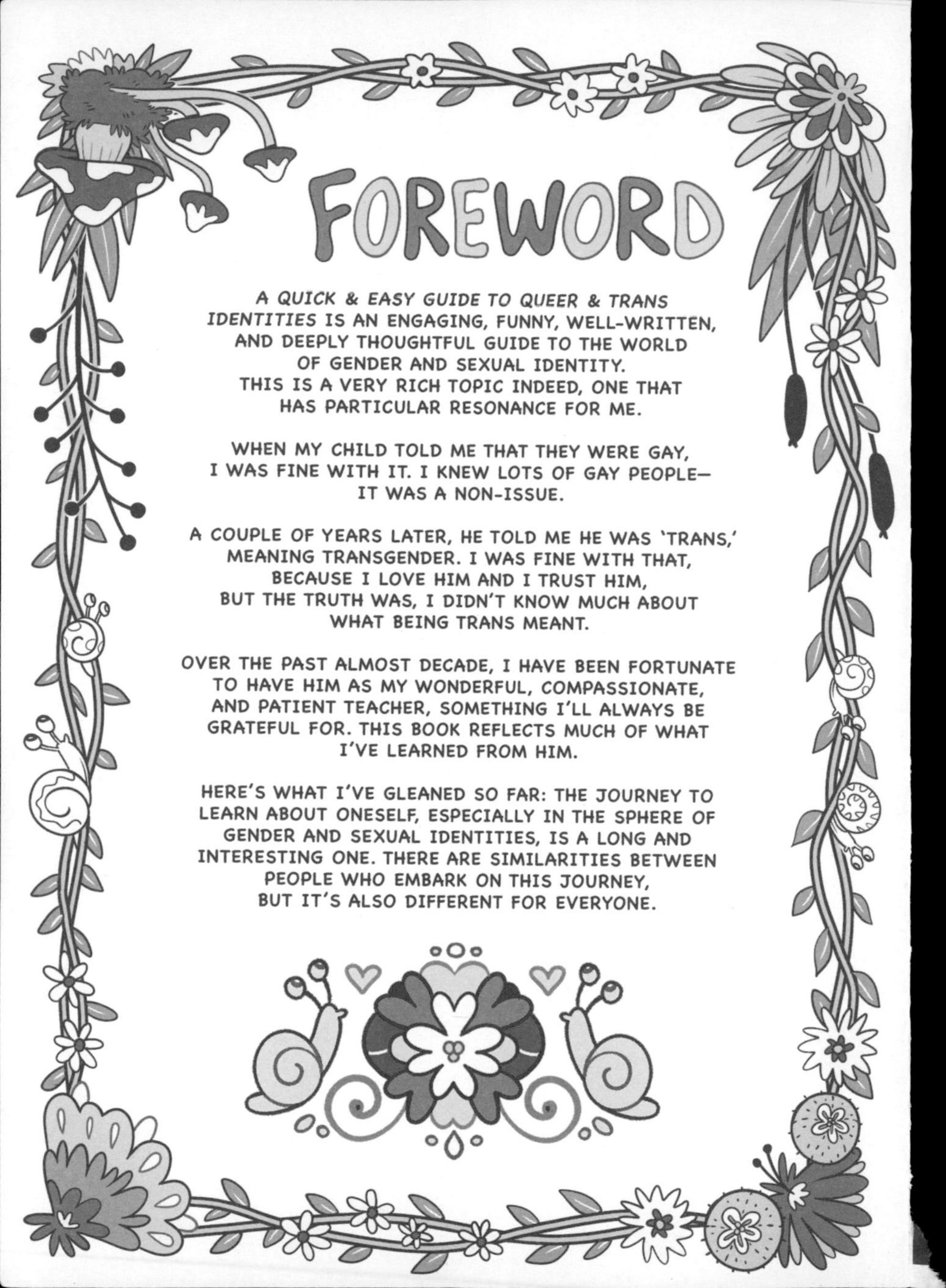

FOREWORD

A QUICK & EASY GUIDE TO QUEER & TRANS IDENTITIES IS AN ENGAGING, FUNNY, WELL-WRITTEN, AND DEEPLY THOUGHTFUL GUIDE TO THE WORLD OF GENDER AND SEXUAL IDENTITY. THIS IS A VERY RICH TOPIC INDEED, ONE THAT HAS PARTICULAR RESONANCE FOR ME.

WHEN MY CHILD TOLD ME THAT THEY WERE GAY, I WAS FINE WITH IT. I KNEW LOTS OF GAY PEOPLE—IT WAS A NON-ISSUE.

A COUPLE OF YEARS LATER, HE TOLD ME HE WAS 'TRANS,' MEANING TRANSGENDER. I WAS FINE WITH THAT, BECAUSE I LOVE HIM AND I TRUST HIM, BUT THE TRUTH WAS, I DIDN'T KNOW MUCH ABOUT WHAT BEING TRANS MEANT.

OVER THE PAST ALMOST DECADE, I HAVE BEEN FORTUNATE TO HAVE HIM AS MY WONDERFUL, COMPASSIONATE, AND PATIENT TEACHER, SOMETHING I'LL ALWAYS BE GRATEFUL FOR. THIS BOOK REFLECTS MUCH OF WHAT I'VE LEARNED FROM HIM.

HERE'S WHAT I'VE GLEANED SO FAR: THE JOURNEY TO LEARN ABOUT ONESELF, ESPECIALLY IN THE SPHERE OF GENDER AND SEXUAL IDENTITIES, IS A LONG AND INTERESTING ONE. THERE ARE SIMILARITIES BETWEEN PEOPLE WHO EMBARK ON THIS JOURNEY, BUT IT'S ALSO DIFFERENT FOR EVERYONE.

WHAT WORKS FOR ONE PERSON MIGHT NOT WORK FOR ANOTHER. EVERYONE HAS THE RIGHT TO FIGURE IT OUT FOR THEMSELVES:
WHAT PRONOUNS THEY WANT TO USE; HOW THEY WANT TO DRESS AND WHETHER THEY WANT TO DRESS LIKE THAT EVERY DAY OR WHETHER THEY LIKE TO MIX IT UP; WHETHER THEY WANT TO TAKE HORMONES OR NOT, AND ALSO HOW MUCH; WHEN THEY WANT TO 'COME OUT' AND HOW THEY WANT TO DO THAT; AND MUCH MORE.
ALSO, DON'T PUT YOURSELF IN A BOX, ESPECIALLY SOMEONE ELSE'S BOX.
LET YOURSELF GROW AND CHANGE AND LEARN— THAT'S WHAT BEING ALIVE IS ALL ABOUT.
-ROZ CHAST
CARTOONIST, AUTHOR, MOTHER

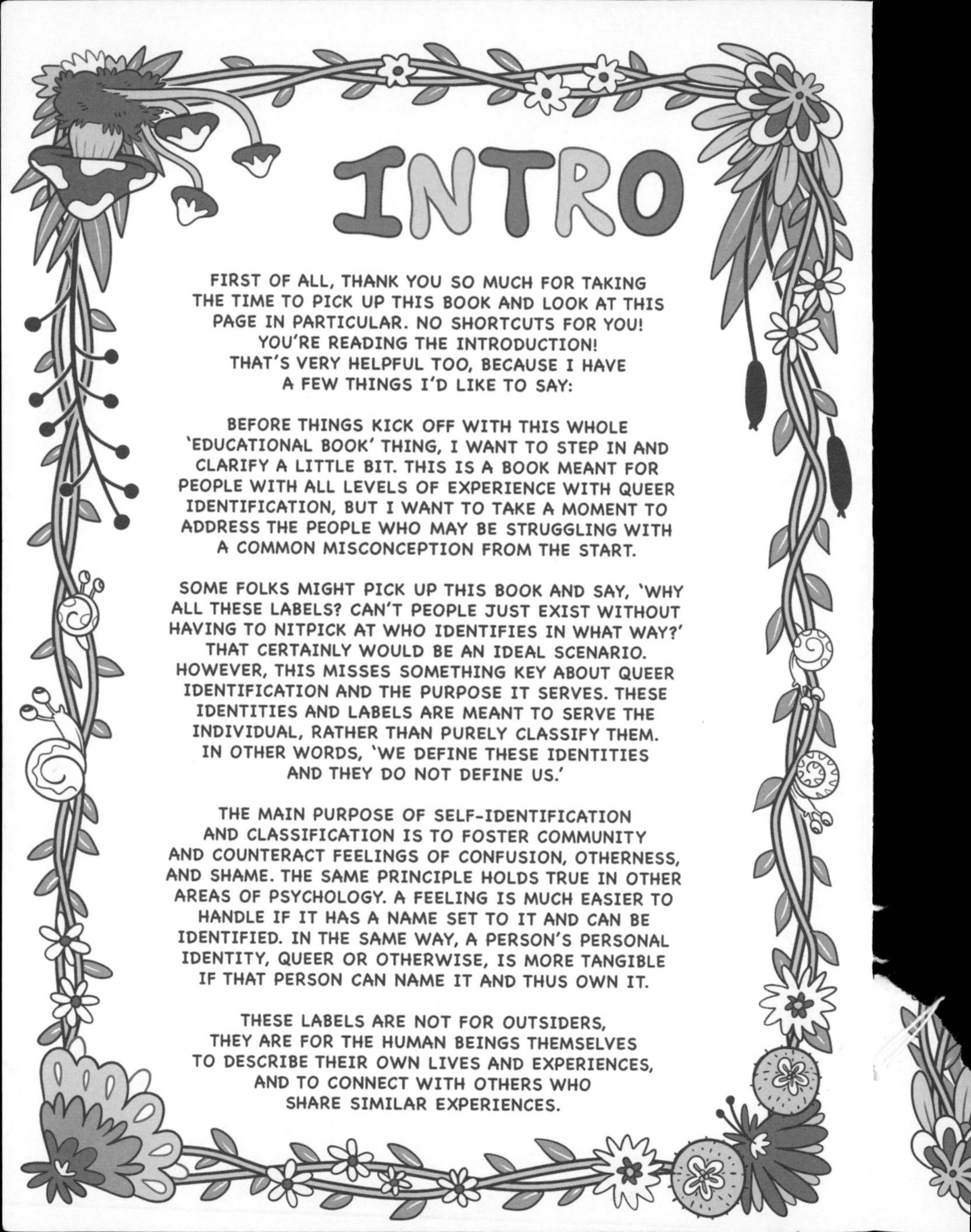

INTRO

FIRST OF ALL, THANK YOU SO MUCH FOR TAKING THE TIME TO PICK UP THIS BOOK AND LOOK AT THIS PAGE IN PARTICULAR. NO SHORTCUTS FOR YOU! YOU'RE READING THE INTRODUCTION! THAT'S VERY HELPFUL TOO, BECAUSE I HAVE A FEW THINGS I'D LIKE TO SAY:

BEFORE THINGS KICK OFF WITH THIS WHOLE 'EDUCATIONAL BOOK' THING, I WANT TO STEP IN AND CLARIFY A LITTLE BIT. THIS IS A BOOK MEANT FOR PEOPLE WITH ALL LEVELS OF EXPERIENCE WITH QUEER IDENTIFICATION, BUT I WANT TO TAKE A MOMENT TO ADDRESS THE PEOPLE WHO MAY BE STRUGGLING WITH A COMMON MISCONCEPTION FROM THE START.

SOME FOLKS MIGHT PICK UP THIS BOOK AND SAY, 'WHY ALL THESE LABELS? CAN'T PEOPLE JUST EXIST WITHOUT HAVING TO NITPICK AT WHO IDENTIFIES IN WHAT WAY?' THAT CERTAINLY WOULD BE AN IDEAL SCENARIO. HOWEVER, THIS MISSES SOMETHING KEY ABOUT QUEER IDENTIFICATION AND THE PURPOSE IT SERVES. THESE IDENTITIES AND LABELS ARE MEANT TO SERVE THE INDIVIDUAL, RATHER THAN PURELY CLASSIFY THEM. IN OTHER WORDS, 'WE DEFINE THESE IDENTITIES AND THEY DO NOT DEFINE US.'

THE MAIN PURPOSE OF SELF-IDENTIFICATION AND CLASSIFICATION IS TO FOSTER COMMUNITY AND COUNTERACT FEELINGS OF CONFUSION, OTHERNESS, AND SHAME. THE SAME PRINCIPLE HOLDS TRUE IN OTHER AREAS OF PSYCHOLOGY. A FEELING IS MUCH EASIER TO HANDLE IF IT HAS A NAME SET TO IT AND CAN BE IDENTIFIED. IN THE SAME WAY, A PERSON'S PERSONAL IDENTITY, QUEER OR OTHERWISE, IS MORE TANGIBLE IF THAT PERSON CAN NAME IT AND THUS OWN IT.

THESE LABELS ARE NOT FOR OUTSIDERS, THEY ARE FOR THE HUMAN BEINGS THEMSELVES TO DESCRIBE THEIR OWN LIVES AND EXPERIENCES, AND TO CONNECT WITH OTHERS WHO SHARE SIMILAR EXPERIENCES.

GROWING UP LONELY, GENDER-AMBIGUOUS, AND WITH A SEXUALITY I DIDN'T UNDERSTAND WAS DIFFICULT. NOWADAYS, YOUNG PEOPLE HAVE THE TOOLS AVAILABLE FOR THEM TO LEARN AND GROW RATHER THAN HIDE AND DESPAIR, AND THAT'S AN AMAZING THING!

IT'S ALSO IMPORTANT TO RECOGNIZE THAT LGBTQ+ LANGUAGE OVERALL, INCLUDING THESE TERMS, IS EVER-EVOLVING AND EVER-CHANGING. GENDERED WORDS CAN BE JUST AS FLUID AS GENDER ITSELF, AND WE HOPE TO BE AS INCLUSIVE AS POSSIBLE WITH HOW WE REPRESENT THOSE WORDS AND IDENTITIES.
IT MAY BE CLICHÉ TO SAY, BUT EVERYBODY IS VALID IN WHO THEY ARE AND HOW THEY IDENTIFY, AND WE HOPE TO HIGHLIGHT THAT IN THE FOLLOWING BOOK.
OUR GOAL IS TO SPREAD LOVE AND ACCEPTANCE, NOT TO OTHER OR EXCLUDE.

SO PLEASE, JOIN US AS WE EXAMINE AND UNPACK A FEW OF THESE CHOICE LABELS AND SEE THEIR ROLES WITHIN THE QUEER COMMUNITY.
WE'RE HAPPY TO HAVE YOU!

– MADY G.

WHO ARE THEY?

I DON'T KNOW. I'VE NEVER SEEN HUMANS LIKE THAT BEFORE....

SO MANY COLORS AND SHAPES!
YOU DON'T THINK THEY'RE POISONOUS... DO YOU?
WHAT ARE ALL THOSE WORDS THEY KEEP SAYING?

POP!

HEEEEEY THERE! WHAT'S UP?
OH! ARE YOU OK, STRANGER?

DID THOSE PRETTY HUMANS CAPTURE YOU?

THE NAME'S IGGY! THIS TANK IS WHERE I LIVE!
WOAH!
SEE THAT HUMAN OVER THERE?

THAT'S MY 'DAD,' BOWERY!
THEY RAISED ME IN HERE AND TAKE REALLY, REALLY GOOD CARE OF ME.

THEY'RE A 'QUEER EDUCATOR' AND BRING ME WITH THEM TO ALL THEIR EVENTS, LIKE THIS ONE HERE!
OOOOH!

WHAT DOES 'QUEER' MEAN? IS THAT WHY THEY'RE ALL SO COLORFUL?

YEAH, THEY DON'T LOOK ANYTHING LIKE THOSE HUNTERS OR GIRL SCOUTS.

NOT NECESSARILY....
QUEERNESS
IS ALL ABOUT HUMAN LOVE AND IDENTITY!
IT'S A LOT MORE COMPLICATED THAN MOST SNAIL STUFF, BUT THAT'S WHAT MAKES IT SO INTERESTING!
WOW! YOU MUST BE SOME KIND OF HUMAN EXPERT OR SOMETHING!
OH, YOU FLATTER ME!

EVERYTHING I KNOW, I LEARNED FROM LISTENING TO BOWERY FROM MY TANK.
HUMANS ARE SO COMPLEX AND AMAZING, I WAS HOOKED RIGHT AWAY!
PARIS IS BURNING
I CAN TEACH YOU SNAILS ALONGSIDE BOWERY'S LESSON IF YOU WANT! I DON'T MIND.
THAT WOULD BE AMAZING!
WE SNAILS DO LOVE TO LEARN!
ALRIGHTY THEN, NEW CURIOUS BUDDIES.
LET'S DIVE ON IN!

WHAT is QUEER?

'QUEER' IS A WORD THAT HAS BEEN USED AS AN INSULT FOR LGBTQ+ PEOPLE SINCE THE TIME OF FAMOUS WRITER AND SOCIALITE OSCAR WILDE— TO WHOM, SOME SAY, IT WAS FIRST USED AGAINST.
WELL, AT LEAST I'M BEING TALKED ABOUT.

TIMES HAVE CHANGED QUITE A BIT SINCE THEN, AND LOTS OF FOLKS HAVE DECIDED TO RECLAIM THE WORD AND USE IT AS SHORTHAND FOR LGBTQ+ AS WELL AS AN UMBRELLA TERM TO COVER ALL DIFFERENT TYPES OF LGBTQ+ IDENTITIES— INCLUDING THOSE WITHOUT A CLEAR NAME.

IT HAS, IN A LOT OF WAYS, TRANSFORMED FROM A SLUR INTO A WORD THAT SYMBOLIZES UNITY AND CAMARADERIE AMONGST 'QUEER' PEOPLE... WHICH IS WHY WE PERSONALLY CHOOSE TO USE IT AS WELL.
QUEER
QUEER
QUEER
PRIDE

EVEN SO, MANY PEOPLE STILL CHOOSE NOT TO USE IT BECAUSE OF ITS HISTORY OF DEROGATORY USE —AND THAT'S OK TOO!
SELF-IDENTIFICATION IS JUST FLEXIBLE LIKE THAT!

ONE OF THE EASIEST WAYS TO START TALKING ABOUT QUEER IDENTITIES IS TO DISCUSS SEXUALITY, AND WHY IT IS A TOTALLY DIFFERENT THING FROM GENDER.
SEXUALITY
GENDER
SOME PEOPLE THINK THAT BEING GAY AND BEING TRANSGENDER MEAN SIMILAR THINGS, AND THAT IS SIMPLY UNTRUE.
I'M SURE YOU'RE ALREADY FAMILIAR WITH THE DIFFERENCE BETWEEN BEING GAY AND BEING STRAIGHT, RIGHT?
ONE IS SAME-GENDER (OR SOMETIMES SAME-'SEX') ATTRACTION—
—AND THE OTHER IS DIFFERENT OR 'OPPOSITE' GENDER ATTRACTION.

BETWEEN THOSE ENDS OF THE SCALE ARE MANY OTHER TYPES OF SEXUALITY. THESE INCLUDE...
BISEXUALITY
ATTRACTION TO THE SAME GENDER AS WELL AS OTHER GENDERS.
ASEXUALITY
A LACK OF SEXUAL ATTRACTION.
PANSEXUALITY
ATTRACTION TO PEOPLE REGARDLESS OF GENDER.
...AND, HONESTLY, MANY OTHERS!
PEOPLE USE LOTS OF DIFFERENT AND UNIQUE TERMS TO DESCRIBE THEIR SEXUALITY.
AFTER ALL, THERE ARE INFINITELY DIFFERENT TYPES OF PEOPLE!
0
1
2
3
4
5
6
HETERO-SEXUAL
AMBI/PAN/BI-SEXUAL
HOMO-SEXUAL
A COMMON WAY OF IDENTIFYING DIFFERENT TYPES OF ATTRACTION LIKE THESE IS VIA THE KINSEY SCALE (DEVELOPED BY DRS. ALFRED KINSEY, WARDELL POMEROY, AND CLYDE MARTIN IN 1948).
IT'S NOT A VERY DETAILED OR PERFECT SCALE, BUT IT'S PRETTY USEFUL IN GAINING THE MOST BASIC UNDERSTANDING OF NON-ASEXUAL SEXUALITIES.

EVEN WITHIN ALL THIS, THERE ARE MANY DIFFERENT TYPES OF SPECIFICALLY ROMANTIC ATTRACTION THAT HAVE NOTHING TO DO WITH SEX AT ALL!
ASEXUAL LOVE IS JUST AS VARIED AND UNIQUE AS SEXUAL LOVE, AS WE'LL GET INTO A BIT LATER.

HOWEVER, ALL THESE DIFFERENT VARIABLES SAY ALMOST NOTHING WHEN DETERMINING A PERSON'S GENDER—AND WHY?
YEAH!
YEAH!
YEAH!
BECAUSE SEXUAL ORIENTATION/ATTRACTION IS DIFFERENT FROM GENDER IDENTITY!
GENDER
NOW, LET'S TAKE A CLOSER LOOK AT WHAT GENDER REALLY MEANS....

WELCOME TO THE HOME OF THE SPROUTLINGS!!
HELLO LI'L TRAVELER!

WHAT'S A SPROUTLING?
WE'RE THE CHILDREN OF THIS FOREST, LIVING HERE SINCE THE FIRST TREES TOOK ROOT.
COME ALONG, WE'LL SHOW YOU AROUND!
HI THERE!

WHILE WE ALL MAY SHARE SOME THINGS IN COMMON, THERE ARE LOTS OF WAYS TO BE A SPROUTLING!
WOAH!
I NEVER KNEW THERE WERE SO MANY WAYS TO BE AND TO LOVE ONE ANOTHER!
I THINK I'LL HANG WITH YOU ALL FOR A BIT!!!

WHAT IS
GENDER
IDENTITY?

GENDER IS THE SOCIAL, CULTURAL, AND MENTAL STATE OF BEING MALE, FEMALE, A COMBINATION OF THE TWO, OR NEITHER. IT HAS TO DO WITH HOW SOMEBODY FEELS INSIDE RATHER THAN WHAT THEY LOOK LIKE.

SEX HAS TO DO WITH REPRODUCTION AS WELL AS PHYSICAL AND BIOLOGICAL MAKE-UP AND CAN REFERENCE THINGS LIKE CHROMOSOMES, GENITALIA, AND HORMONAL ACTIVITY RATHER THAN MENTAL ATTRIBUTES.

HISTORIANS AND BIOLOGISTS SUCH AS ACTIVIST JULIA SERANO AND SCIENCE JOURNALIST CLAIRE AINSWORTH ARE FINDING THAT THE SHEER NUMBER OF VARIABLES INVOLVED IN DETERMINING SOMEBODY'S SEX CAN BE VERY INCONSISTENT, AND IT WOULD BE FAR MORE ACCURATE TO CLASSIFY PEOPLE BY USING THOSE INDIVIDUAL VARIABLES INSTEAD.
CHROMOSOMES, HORMONES, GENITALIA, AND INTERNAL ANATOMY CAN VARY IN SO MANY DIFFERENT WAYS THAT LUMPING PEOPLE INTO 'MALE' AND 'FEMALE' SEXES DOESN'T MAKE MUCH BIOLOGICAL SENSE FOR HUMANS.

TRANSGENDER FOLKS OFTEN USE TERMS LIKE 'ASSIGNED SEX' OR 'DESIGNATED SEX' TO DESCRIBE HOW A PERSON HAS BEEN REFERRED TO AT BIRTH RATHER THAN JUST THE WORD 'SEX' ON ITS OWN.
AFAB
ASSIGNED FEMALE AT BIRTH
AMAB
ASSIGNED MALE AT BIRTH
THIS LANGUAGE IS MORE APPROPRIATE AND MORE RESPECTFUL TO THOSE WHOSE ASSIGNED SEX DOES NOT ALIGN WITH THEIR GENDER.
A PERSON WHOSE ASSIGNED SEX AND GENDER MATCH WOULD BE 'CISGENDER.'
A PERSON'S WHOSE ASSIGNED SEX AND GENDER DO NOT MATCH WOULD BE 'TRANSGENDER.'

THESE SPECTRUM DESIGNS BOTH HAVE ONE COMMONALITY, HOWEVER:

THE INCLUSION OF BINARY MALE AND BINARY FEMALE GENDERS AS A BASELINE.

IF A PERSON IDENTIFIES SOLELY AS MALE OR FEMALE, THAT WOULD MEAN THEY HAVE A BINARY GENDER.

NON-BINARY PEOPLE CAN HAVE GENDERS THAT GO ALL OVER THE SPECTRUM AND CAN EVEN REJECT THAT SPECTRUM COMPLETELY.
THERE ARE INFINITE COMBINATIONS OF MALE AND FEMALE THAT CAN BE FELT AND EXPRESSED AS WELL AS THE COMPLETE LACK OF GENDER ALTOGETHER.
PEOPLE WHO FEEL THAT THEY DO NOT HAVE A GENDER, LIKE BOWERY, ARE OFTEN KNOWN AS 'AGENDER' PEOPLE, OR 'NEUTROIS' IF YOU WANT TO BE FRENCH AND FANCY.
SOME FEEL MORE 'GENDER-FULL,' SOME FEEL MORE 'GENDERLESS,' SOME FEEL 'GENDERFLUID'— BUT EVERYBODY PRETTY MUCH JUST WANTS TO LIVE THEIR LIVES.
SELF-LABELING IN THESE WAYS CAN HELP A PERSON FEEL MORE GROUNDED IN THEIR IDENTITY AS WELL AS FIND OTHER PEOPLE WITH SIMILAR EMOTIONS AND EXPERIENCES.
THE WORLD IS HOME TO SUCH A VIBRANT RAINBOW OF PEOPLE, SO WHY NOT GENDERS?

CAN I SHARE SOMETHING WITH YOU?
SURE.

I'VE ALWAYS ADMIRED HOW COMFORTABLE YOU ARE IN YOUR SELF-IMAGE AND IDENTITY. IT'S REALLY GIVEN ME CONFIDENCE AND INSPIRATION.

HONESTLY, I'M NOT QUITE SURE WHO I AM ENTIRELY!

I'VE COME A LONG WAY, BUT THIS JOURNEY IS FAR FROM OVER.

IT MAY NEVER BE. AND THAT'S OKAY!
I HAD NO iDEA YOU FELT THAT WAY.

Now ... WHAT'S
GENDER
EXPRESSION?

FOR AGES WE'VE BEEN TAUGHT
THAT THERE ARE 'BOY THINGS'
AND 'GIRL THINGS.'
THIS LOGIC IS FLAWED OVERALL,
BUT HERE WE'RE GOING
TO FOCUS ON APPEARANCE.
MOST PEOPLE WILL AGREE THAT
THERE ARE CLASSICALLY
'FEMALE' AND 'MALE' TYPES OF
CLOTHING—BUT WHY MUST
THAT BE THE CASE?

SOCIETY
SOCIETY
Society
IT ALL COMES DOWN TO NOTHING
BUT SOCIETAL EXPECTATIONS,
REALLY....

WE'VE ALREADY DISCUSSED THE GENDER SPECTRUM, SO YOU CAN PROBABLY GUESS THAT GENDER EXPRESSION CAN FIT WITHIN THE SAME MATRIX.
A PERSON CAN DRESS IN A CLASSICALLY 'FEMININE' OR 'MASCULINE' WAY, AS WELL AS IN A MORE NEUTRAL OR 'ANDROGYNOUS' WAY.
THESE AESTHETICS CAN BE CHANGED OR COMBINED IN ANY WAY SOMEBODY FEELS FITS THEIR PERSONALITY.

THERE ARE ALSO A MYRIAD OF DIFFERENT GENDER PRESENTATIONS THAT PLAY WITH THESE SOCIETAL BOUNDARIES, SUCH AS...
HARD Femme
Soft BUTCH
Soft MASC
PLAYING WITH THESE TYPES OF LABELS AND PRESENTATION HAS BEEN A HALLMARK OF QUEER CULTURE FOR CENTURIES (PARTICULARLY LESBIAN CULTURE), AND HAS ALSO SERVED AS A WAY TO IDENTIFY EACH OTHER WITHIN QUEER SUB-COMMUNITIES.
BUTCH FOREST
Femme GARDENS
EXPERIMENTATION WITH ONE'S APPEARANCE CAN BE VERY FREEING AND VALIDATING, AND THOSE FEELINGS ARE FINALLY BEING VALUED MORE THAN A PRE-CONSTRUCTED SET OF LIMITING EXPECTATIONS.
IT'S A FAIRLY SIMPLE WAY TO TAKE CONTROL OF AND AFFIRM ONE'S OWN GENDER OR SEXUALITY.

THE FEELING OF A BRA STRAP AROUND MY RIBS OR MY GIRLY UNDERWEAR RIDING UP WOULD MAKE ME FEEL LIKE I'M WEARING SANDPAPER INSTEAD.
NOW THAT I'VE SWITCHED TO UNDERGARMENTS THAT I'M MORE HAPPY SEEING MYSELF IN, I'VE REALIZED THAT MY AWARENESS OF THOSE REGIONS OF MY BODY WERE WHAT WAS CAUSING MY DISCOMFORT.
GENDER EXPRESSION DOESN'T ALWAYS ALIGN WITH A PERSON'S GENDER IDENTITY, BUT IT CAN OFTEN BE USED AS A CLUE TO HOW A PERSON WOULD LIKE TO BE ADDRESSED.
THAT BEING SAID, IT'S ALWAYS BEST TO ASK IF THE SITUATION ALLOWS FOR IT, AND PRONOUN USAGE CAN BE EASY TO CORRECT WHEN PROMPTED.

THE WORLD HAS PLENTY OF FEMININE MEN, MASCULINE WOMEN, AND EVERYBODY IN BETWEEN. JUST BE POLITE AND RESPECTFUL, IT'S NOT THAT HARD!

HOWEVER, NOT EVERY PLACE IS CREATED EQUAL AS FAR AS SAFETY IN EXPRESSION GOES....

THERE MAY BE TIMES IN WHICH PEOPLE ARE FORCED TO STICK TO OUTDATED SOCIETAL EXPECTATIONS IN ORDER TO APPEASE OTHERS OR EVEN PRESERVE THEIR OWN HEALTH AND WELLBEING IN A POTENTIALLY DANGEROUS ENVIRONMENT.
THIS DOESN'T INVALIDATE A PERSON'S EMOTIONS OR IDENTITY. IT'S ALL ABOUT SURVIVAL. WE MUST ALL USE OUR BEST JUDGEMENT.
IF YOU WANT TO EXPERIMENT WITH YOUR OWN GENDER PRESENTATION, A GOOD WAY TO START IS ON HOLIDAYS LIKE HALLOWEEN OR AT FANCY-DRESS PARTIES.
COSTUMED OCCASIONS CAN BE A GREAT GATEWAY INTO EXPERIMENTING WITH ONE'S PERSONAL APPEARANCE WITHOUT ATTRACTING TOO MUCH ATTENTION—ESPECIALLY UNWANTED NEGATIVE ATTENTION THAT CAN COME FROM MORE JUDGMENTAL OR BIGOTED PEOPLE.

HERE'S A SIGNIFICANT MEMORY FROM A FRIEND TO ADD A LITTLE PERSPECTIVE....

FOURTH OF JULY WEEKEND,
2011 OR 2012, I FORGET WHICH....

(M) AND I HAD GONE TO SPEND THE HOLIDAY WITH HER EXTENDED FAMILY, AND CLOSETED-ME PACKED EXCLUSIVELY FEMMY CLOTHES...

...EXCEPT BOXERS AND A BIG T-SHIRT TO SLEEP IN.

ONE OF HER MALE COUSINS PROCEEDED TO INAPPROPRIATELY COME ON TO ME, CREATING AN INHOSPITABLE ENVIRONMENT FOR ME, (M), AND HONESTLY EVERYONE THERE.

WE GRACEFULLY BOWED OUT EARLY TO CELEBRATE/ESCAPE ON OUR OWN, BACK AT HER HOUSE.

AS SOON AS WE ARRIVED,
I REMEMBER, CLEAR AS DAY,
TURNING TO (M) AND SAYING...

...NOW THAT WE'RE
HERE, ALONE,
I CAN BE MYSELF—
A GOSH-DANG
GENTLEMAN.

I CHANGED OUT OF MY SKIRT AND TANK TOP AND INTO MY BOXERS AND TEE, AND THE FEELING THAT FOLLOWED WAS SUCH SECURE, INDESCRIBABLE, 'BECOMING-WHOLE' BLISS.

I COULDN'T PLACE IT AT THE TIME, BUT I'D BE CHASING THAT FEELING AGAIN FOR YEARS TO COME.

WANNA GO TO THE DANCE TONIGHT? EVERYONE'S GONNA BE THERE!!
I DO, BUT... MY LEAVES ARE SO LONG AND FLAT. I LOOK LIKE A WEEPING WILLOW!

HOW ABOUT WE TRY OUT SOME NEW LOOKS?
OH... OK!!!

LOOKIN' GOOD, FERN!!
I DUNNO

THIS ONE ACTUALLY... FEELS GOOD!
LET'S GO.

HEY FERN!! WANNA DANCE WITH ME?

YOU LOOK SO HANDSOME TONIGHT!
THANKS! I'VE... NEVER FELT THIS WAY BEFORE.

WHAT DOES
DYSPHORIA
MEAN?

INHABITING A BODY THAT DOESN'T ALIGN WITH THEIR GENDER CAN CAUSE PEOPLE QUITE A BIT OF MENTAL ANGUISH.
'GENDER DYSPHORIA' IS THE TERM USED TO DESCRIBE THE NEGATIVE OR UNCOMFORTABLE EMOTIONS MANY TRANSGENDER PEOPLE FEEL REGARDING THEIR BODIES OR APPEARANCE.
NOT EVERY TRANS PERSON EXPERIENCES DYSPHORIA, AND IT VARIES FROM PERSON TO PERSON.
'DYSPHORIA,' AS A WORD, IS THE OPPOSITE OF 'EUPHORIA,' MEANING BLISS AND HAPPINESS.

THIS IS APPROPRIATE, CONSIDERING HOW SEVERE AND DEPRESSING GENDER DYSPHORIA CAN BE.

PHYSICAL DYSPHORIA REFERS TO DISSATISFACTION WITH ONE'S OWN BODY.

A TYPE OF DYSPHORIA THAT HAS ONLY RECENTLY BEGUN TO BE DISCUSSED IS NON-BINARY DYSPHORIA.
DYSPHORIA CAN MANIFEST IN SOME UNIQUE WAYS FOR SOME NON-BINARY PEOPLE THAT MIGHT NOT BE SHARED BY THOSE WITH BINARY GENDERS.
LEVELS OF DYSPHORIA CAN SHIFT MORE FLUIDLY AND CAN INCLUDE DYSPHORIA ABOUT HAVING A HUMAN BODY, PERIOD.
SOME (NOT ALL) NON-BINARY PEOPLE FEEL SOME KIND OF CONNECTION WITH NON-HUMAN CHARACTERS BECAUSE THEY FEEL THOSE THINGS ARE 'LESS GENDERED' THAN A HUMAN BODY.

FOR THIS REASON, THOSE KINDS OF NON-BINARY PEOPLE PARTICULARLY ENJOY THINGS LIKE ALIENS, ROBOTS, AND OTHER NON-HUMAN REPRESENTATIONS.
IT'S NOT UNCOMMON FOR TRANSGENDER PEOPLE OF ALL TYPES TO IDENTIFY WITH SOME NON-HUMAN AVATAR, BUT IT'S PARTICULARLY COMMON FOR YOUNGER NON-BINARY TRANS PEOPLE.

*BINDING SAFETY IS IMPORTANT! DO NOT USE BANDAGES!

THE MOST BASIC WAY TO COMBAT DYSPHORIA IS TO WORK ON HOW YOU SEE YOURSELF.

LEARNING TO LOVE YOURSELF AS YOU ARE IS PROBABLY THE MOST IMPORTANT PART OF TRANSITIONING, WHETHER YOU CHOOSE TO MEDICALLY TRANSITION OR NOT.

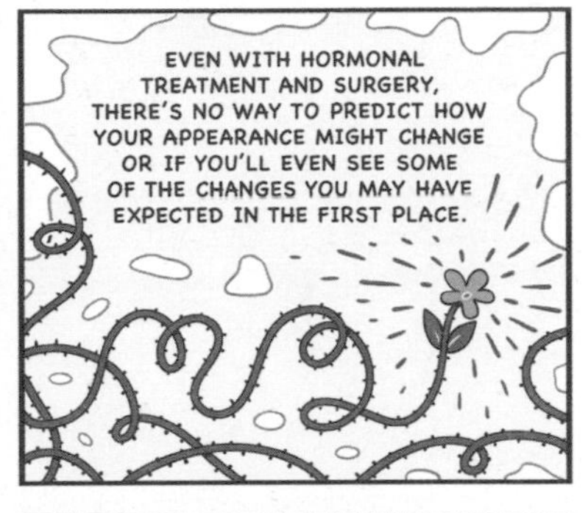
EVEN WITH HORMONAL TREATMENT AND SURGERY, THERE'S NO WAY TO PREDICT HOW YOUR APPEARANCE MIGHT CHANGE OR IF YOU'LL EVEN SEE SOME OF THE CHANGES YOU MAY HAVE EXPECTED IN THE FIRST PLACE.

A SELF-IMAGE BOOST CAN MAKE A HUGE DIFFERENCE, BE IT A CHANGE IN CLOTHING, HAIRSTYLE, OR MAKEUP. A LITTLE CAN GO A LONG WAY AS FAR AS BASIC COSMETIC CHANGES GO.

IT'S SO EASY TO FIND FLAWS IN ONE'S OWN APPEARANCE THAT WE CAN GET LOST IN IT, BUT TRY TO TAKE A STEP BACK AND REMEMBER THAT YOU ARE YOU AND THAT'S ALL YOU CAN BE. SOME THINGS WON'T EVER BE 'PERFECT,' BUT THAT'S JUST THE WAY LIFE IS.

EVERY PERSON IS WORTHWHILE AND VALUABLE IN THEIR OWN WAY, AND IF YOU ARE ABLE TO MAKE SOME SORT OF PEACE WITH YOURSELF WHILE ON YOUR TRANSITIONAL JOURNEY, THAT WILL DEFINITELY EASE THE BURDEN.

I KNOW I'M ON MY GENDER JOURNEY BECAUSE I NOTICE MYSELF GETTING MORE AND MORE CONTENT WITH WHAT I'M SEEING IN THE MIRROR, BUT I STILL HAVE TO PUT A CONCERTED EFFORT INTO THE AESTHETIC PACKAGE TO BE OK GOING OUT IN PUBLIC.

I'D LIKE TO BE COMFORTABLE ENOUGH IN MY BODY TO GO TO THE BEACH AND FEEL AS AT HOME THERE AS MY CIS PEERS.
I'M TRUSTING MY GUT MORE, TRYING TO FOCUS LESS ON WHAT OTHERS ARE DOING, AND MORE ON WHAT FEELS RIGHT TO ME.

FOR ME PERSONALLY, SOME FORM OF TOP SURGERY IS IN MY FUTURE.
I'D REALLY LOVE TO HAVE A DOCTOR OR SOME GENDER PROFESSIONAL IN MY LIFE WHO I CAN GROW TO TRUST AND WHO CAN HELP GUIDE MY DECISIONS SAFELY TOWARDS MY GOAL.

I THINK I FEEL LESS DYSPHORIC WHEN I FEEL MORE ATTRACTIVE.
LIKE, EVEN WHEN I SEE MYSELF AS BEING AN ATTRACTIVE BOY, I FEEL OK BECAUSE I CAN SEE HOW I COULD EASILY TRANSITION INTO BEING MORE VISIBLY FEMININE.

I DON'T FIND MYSELF RELATING TO FICTIONAL CHARACTERS AS MUCH AS I SEE OTHER PEOPLE DO, SO SEEING REAL TRANS FEMMES ONLINE IS THE BEST FOR ME.

I THINK JUST TALKING TO GIRLS, WEARING FEMME CLOTHING, AND BEING MORE TRADITIONALLY FEMME SEXUALLY, ARE SOME MORE GENERAL THINGS THAT HELP ME WITH DYSPHORIA.

SEEING OTHER HAPPY TRANS WOMEN IS REALLY NICE!

STARTING OUT, IT WAS INCREDIBLY DISCOURAGING TO NOT HAVE ANY TRANS ROLE MODELS WHO LOOKED OR ACTED LIKE ME.

I'M NOT GOING TO PRETEND IT'S NOT DIFFICULT, BUT EVERY DAY I STRIVE TO BE MY OWN ROLE MODEL.

SIMPLY BY BEING TRANS, YOU DEFINE ITS MEANING. YOU ARE ENOUGH.

TRY AND MAKE THE DECISIONS THAT MAKE YOU HAPPY AND COMFORTABLE.
DON'T WASTE TIME TRYING TO FIT INTO SOMEONE ELSE'S DEFINITION OF WHO YOU SHOULD BE.

IT'S ALSO VERY IMPORTANT TO NOT COMPARE YOURSELF TOO MUCH TO CIS WOMEN/MEN—OTHER THAN THINGS LIKE FASHION OR STYLE...

...INSTEAD, FOCUS ON SUPPORTING OTHER TRANS FOLKS AND TRYING TO BE THE BEST YOU THAT YOU CAN!
TRANS

LIVING YOUR OWN BEST LIFE CAN REALLY HELP IMPROVE THE LIVES OF OTHERS!

I'VE ALWAYS LONGED FOR BRIGHT BLUE FLOWERS THAT BLOOM IN THE SPRING.

I LOOKED FOR AN ANSWER IN THE TREES.

THE SUN.

THE MINERAL RICH WATER.

IT'S BEEN MONTHS, BUT IT FEELS LONGER.

THE CHANGES ARE SMALL,
BUT I'M BEGINNING
TO SEE THEM.

SO, WHAT IS
ASEXUALITY?

LOTS OF PEOPLE EXPERIENCE SEXUAL ATTRACTION, BUT THERE ARE ALSO PLENTY OF PEOPLE WHO DON'T. THIS IS ASEXUALITY, AS WELL AS THE ASEXUAL SPECTRUM OF IDENTITY.

ASEXUALITY, IN THE MOST BASIC TERMS, IS A LACK OF SEXUAL ATTRACTION.
XXX
SNAIL HUNKS
???

THAT BEING SAID, NOT EVERY ASEXUAL PERSON EXPERIENCES THEIR ASEXUALITY THE SAME WAY.

ASEXUAL (ace)
SEX-REPULSED
CELIBATE
IT'S ALSO IMPORTANT TO HIGHLIGHT THE DISTINCTION BETWEEN ASEXUALITY, CELIBACY, AND SEXUAL REPULSION.
CHOICE
CELIBATE
SEX-REPULSED
PSYCHOLOGICAL
ASEXUAL
SEXUALITY
CELIBACY IS A CHOICE TO NOT BE SEXUALLY ACTIVE, WHILE ASEXUALITY IS A SEXUALITY AND NOT A CHOICE...

...SEXUAL REPULSION CAN RESULT IN A LACK OF INTEREST IN SEX, BUT IS GENERALLY CAUSED BY A PAST EXPERIENCE OR TRAUMA, UNLIKE ASEXUALITY WHICH, ONCE AGAIN, IS AN ORIENTATION.
SEXUAL REPULSION

SOME ASEXUAL PEOPLE STILL HAVE THE DESIRE FOR ROMANTIC, PARTNERED RELATIONSHIPS...

...WHILE SOME MIGHT FEEL MORE COMFORTABLE WITH NO RELATIONSHIP LIKE THAT AT ALL.

SOME PREFER SOLITUDE, SOME PREFER CLOSE FRIENDSHIPS. ASEXUALITY IS JUST AS NUANCED AS ANY OTHER TYPE OF SEXUALITY, IF NOT MORE-SO!

ASEXUAL PEOPLE WILL OFTEN STILL IDENTIFY WITH A SECONDARY ORIENTATION, WHICH USUALLY ADDRESSES THEIR ROMANTIC INTERESTS.
BI
PAN
GAY
HET

THERE ARE ASEXUALS WHO ARE 'HETEROROMANTIC,' 'HOMOROMANTIC,' 'BIROMANTIC,' AND SO-ON.

THAT BEING SAID, THERE ARE PLENTY OF ASEXUALS OUT THERE WHO JUST DON'T REALLY FEEL ANY TYPE OF ROMANTIC ATTRACTION EITHER. THIS IS KNOWN AS BEING AN 'AROMANTIC' ASEXUAL OR 'ARO/ACE,' TO USE POPULAR ABBREVIATIONS.
SNOMIX

ADDITIONALLY, JUST BECAUSE A PERSON IS ASEXUAL, DOESN'T MEAN THAT THEY DO NOT EXPERIENCE SEXUAL AROUSAL.
PLENTY OF ASEXUAL PEOPLE STILL MASTURBATE OR EVEN HAVE SEX WITH THEIR PARTNERS.
DO NOT DISTURB

AROUSAL IS SEPARATE FROM ATTRACTION IN THIS WAY BECAUSE OF ITS NATURE AS A PHYSICAL REFLEX.

A PERSON CAN BE ASEXUAL AND STILL HAVE A HIGH LIBIDO, JUST LIKE A PERSON CAN BE NON-ASEXUAL AND HAVE A LOW LIBIDO.
LIBIDO
XXX

WITHIN THE SPECTRUM OF ASEXUAL IDENTITY, THERE ARE MANY VARIATIONS AND COMBINATIONS OF ASEXUALITY AND SEXUALITY:

THERE ARE 'DEMISEXUAL' PEOPLE WHO TEND TO REQUIRE A DEEPER AND MORE INTIMATE RELATIONSHIP WITH A PERSON IN ORDER TO FEEL SEXUAL ATTRACTION.
XXX
THERE ARE 'CUPIOSEXUAL,' 'PLACIOSEXUAL,' AND 'LITHOSEXUAL' PEOPLE WHO DESIRE A SEXUAL RELATIONSHIP WITH SOMEBODY, EVEN THOUGH THEY ARE NOT SEXUALLY ATTRACTED TO THEM.

THERE ARE 'AUTOCHORISSEXUAL' PEOPLE WHO FEEL SEXUAL ATTRACTION, BUT ONLY IN SCENARIOS THAT DON'T INVOLVE THEIR OWN PARTICIPATION.

THERE ARE EVEN 'GREY ASEXUAL' PEOPLE WHO GENERALLY DO NOT FEEL SEXUAL ATTRACTION, BUT HAVE A FEW EXCEPTIONS OR PERSONAL LIMITATIONS.

THE ASEXUALITY SPECTRUM EXISTS FOR THE SAKE OF INCLUSIVITY.
THERE ARE NO ASEXUAL 'GATEKEEPERS' AND PLENTY OF ROOM FOR ALL TYPES OF ASEXUALITY UNDER THE UMBRELLA!

A HALLMARK OF MOST ASEXUAL RELATIONSHIPS IS NON-SEXUAL INTIMACY.
THIS CAN BE IN THE FORM OF KISSES, HUGS, CUDDLES, NON-SEXUAL TOUCHING, AND MUCH MORE.

SOME NON-PHYSICAL ACTS CAN PRODUCE STRONG FEELINGS OF INTIMACY AS WELL, SUCH AS COOKING FOR SOMEBODY OR PLAYING MUSIC.

ASEXUAL RELATIONSHIPS, LIKE ALL HEALTHY RELATIONSHIPS, HAVE A FOUNDATION OF MUTUAL RESPECT, INTEREST, INTIMACY (WHATEVER THAT MAY REPRESENT), AND FUN!

ASEXUALITY HAS ONLY RECENTLY BEEN REALLY GIVEN THE ATTENTION IT DESERVES IN SCIENCE AND MEDIA, AND AS A RESULT, MORE AND MORE INFORMATION ABOUT IT IS AND WILL CONTINUE TO BE AVAILABLE.
IT'S A DIVERSE AND COMPLEX SPECTRUM OF IDENTITIES THAT COULD CERTAINLY BENEFIT FROM THESE INCREASED LEVELS OF INTEREST AND UNDERSTANDING.

I COULD EASILY SPEND ALL DAY HERE... I LIKE YOU A LOT.

I REALLY LIKE YOU TOO, BUT IN THE FRIEND KIND OF WAY.

THAT'S OKAY, BUD! IF YOU HAVE FEELINGS FOR SOMEONE ELSE, I WON'T BE HURT.

I DON'T! HAVING PALS I CAN BE COZY AND TALK WITH IS JUST RIGHT FOR ME.

WELL, YOU'RE A REALLY IMPORTANT FRIEND TO ME.

WHAT DOES IT MEAN TO
COME OUT?

COMING OUT IS GENERALLY A VERY IMPORTANT MOMENT IN AN LGBTQ+ PERSON'S LIFE. IT'S SEEN AS A TIME OF REBIRTH, WHEN THE PERSON CAN FINALLY EXPRESS WHO THEY REALLY ARE INSIDE.

WHILE TRUE FOR MOST GAY, BI, OR PAN FOLKS, THIS CAN BE ESPECIALLY TRUE FOR TRANSGENDER INDIVIDUALS.
?

COMING OUT AS A TRANS PERSON IS THE BEGINNING OF A VERY INTIMATE AND OFTEN PHYSICAL JOURNEY THAT PLAYS A MONUMENTAL ROLE IN ONE'S HAPPINESS.

*AUTHOR'S NOTE: LGBTQ+ 'BALL CULTURE' WAS PIONEERED MAINLY BY TRANS PEOPLE OF COLOR.

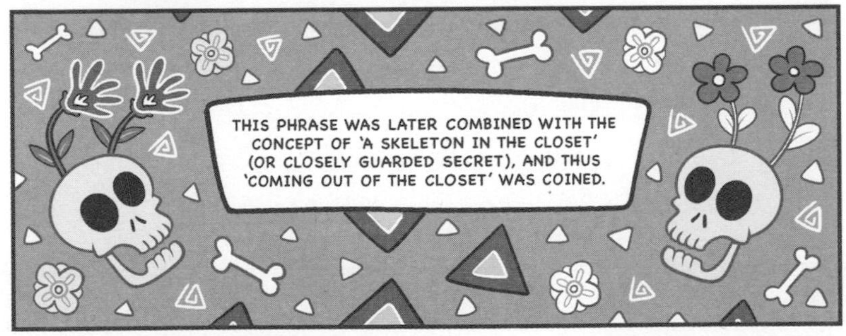

COMING OUT IS ALSO A PRIVILEGE. THERE ARE MANY ENVIRONMENTS IN WHICH A PERSON MAY NOT FEEL SAFE EXPOSING SUCH INTIMATE DETAILS ABOUT THEMSELF.

THIS COULD BE IN A WORK ENVIRONMENT, AMONGST JUDGMENTAL PEERS, OR WITH CLOSED-MINDED FAMILY MEMBERS.

BEING EXPOSED TO OR REJECTED BY THESE PEOPLE IS VERY PAINFUL, AND SOMETIMES LGBTQ+ FOLKS WILL REMAIN 'CLOSETED' TO AVOID SUCH CONFRONTATION OR UNWANTED CONSEQUENCES (SUCH AS LOSS OF HOUSING OR ABANDONMENT).

IF SOMEBODY IS TAKING THEIR TIME COMING OUT, IT'S PROBABLY FOR AN IMPORTANT REASON. A PERSON ALSO MIGHT CHOOSE TO ONLY BE OUT TO FRIENDS AND NOT THEIR FAMILY OR CO-WORKERS.

AS FAR AS 'COMING OUT TECHNIQUE' GOES, THERE IS NO REAL RIGHT OR WRONG ANSWER, AND EVERYTHING DEPENDS ON A PERSON'S SITUATION. THIS BEING SAID, THERE ARE DEFINITELY A FEW THINGS TO KEEP IN MIND:
1
SELF RESPECT
YOU CANNOT CONTROL ANYBODY'S REACTIONS, BUT YOU CAN CONTROL HOW YOU CONFRONT THOSE REACTIONS.
KEEP YOUR HEAD HELD HIGH, UNDERSTAND THAT THERE IS NOTHING 'WRONG' WITH YOU AND THAT YOU DESERVE LOVE AND RESPECT, NO MATTER THE OUTCOME OF THIS 'BIG REVEAL.'
THE EXPERIENCE MAY BE ROUGH OR IT MAY BE GREAT, BUT YOU WILL ALWAYS BE WHO YOU ARE AND YOU OWN THAT.
2
STEREOTYPES & ROLES
WHEN YOU COME OUT, YOU MAY BE TEMPTED TO RUSH INTO ANOTHER 'EXPECTED' ROLE AND TRY TO CHANGE YOURSELF INTO SOMEBODY YOU THINK YOU 'SHOULD BE.'
AN EXAMPLE OF THIS COULD BE A TRANS WOMAN PRESSURING HERSELF TO BE MORE 'GIRLY' OR A TRANS MAN REJECTING ALL 'FEMININE' THINGS EVEN THOUGH HE STILL ENJOYS SOME OF THEM.

SIMILAR PRESSURES ARE ALSO PUT ON GAY AND LESBIAN PEOPLE, SUCH AS STEREOTYPICAL EXPECTATIONS OF VANITY AND PROMISCUITY OR CLASSICALLY 'FEMME' OR 'BUTCH' BEHAVIORS.
THERE'S NO RIGHT OR WRONG WAY TO BE GAY, STRAIGHT, MALE, FEMALE, OR WHATEVER YOU ARE. DON'T PUT YOURSELF IN ANOTHER BOX. YOU JUST CAME OUT OF ONE!
3
PREPARATION & ADAPTATION
THERE IS NO WAY TO KNOW HOW THINGS WILL GO BEFORE YOU ACTUALLY COME OUT, BUT YOU CAN ALWAYS PREPARE FOR LIKELY OUTCOMES.
PROS
CONS
DO YOU HAVE FRIENDS/FAMILY MEMBERS WHO WILL SUPPORT YOU? WHO CAN YOU COUNT ON IF THINGS GO SOUR? ARE YOU COMFORTABLE WITH YOURSELF BEFOREHAND? HOW MUCH ARE YOU PREPARED TO EDUCATE PEOPLE?
THESE ARE ALL IMPORTANT QUESTIONS TO CONSIDER BEFORE COMING OUT, AND BEING ABLE TO ADAPT TO MULTIPLE OUTCOMES WILL BE A BIG ADVANTAGE BOTH IN COMING OUT AND IN LIFE OVERALL.

4
NO NEED TO RUSH
A SAFE AND MORE COMFORTABLE WAY TO START WOULD PROBABLY BE TO TRY COMING OUT TO ONE VERY CLOSE FRIEND, AND EVENTUALLY BRANCHING OUT INTO BEING MORE PUBLIC.
COMING OUT CAN BE A LENGTHY PROCESS FOR SOME AND MIGHT EVOLVE AS LIFE GOES ON. A PERSON MIGHT FIND THEIR PERSONAL LABELS FLUCTUATING AND WANT TO COME OUT MULTIPLE TIMES FOR DIFFERENT THINGS—LIKE SOMEBODY WHO COMES OUT AS BI AS WELL AS TRANS.
THIS IS VERY NORMAL, AND A PERSON'S CONNECTION WITH THEIR SEXUAL OR GENDER IDENTITY MAY NEVER FULLY SETTLE.
ONCE AGAIN, EVERYBODY IS DIFFERENT AND THAT'S ONE OF THE THINGS THAT MAKES THE LGBTQ+ COMMUNITY SO VIBRANT!

ALL THIS INFORMATION CAN SOUND A LITTLE SCARY, BUT IT DOESN'T HAVE TO BE THAT WAY.
NO MATTER THE OUTCOME OR WHATEVER DECISION YOU MAKE, YOU WILL GROW AND BLOSSOM INTO WHO YOU'RE MEANT TO BE AND THAT'S AN AMAZING THING.

TRY NEW THINGS, TAKE SOME CHANCES. YOU MIGHT BE SURPRISED AT WHAT YOU DISCOVER AND WHAT FEELS 'RIGHT'!

I... HAD WAY MORE FUN AT THE DANCE THAN I THOUGHT I WOULD!

YEAH, I WAS SURPRISED AND EXCITED TO SEE YOU SO HAPPY AND CAREFREE!

I FELT MORE MYSELF THAN EVER! I'M NOT SURE IF I'M READY TO TELL ANYONE, BUT I THINK THIS IS WHO I WANNA BE FROM NOW ON. A FULLER, CURLIER FERN!

THANKS FOR TRUSTING ME, CURLYFERN. TAKE THE TIME YOU NEED. MEANWHILE, LET ME KNOW IF YOU WANT TO TALK ABOUT IT MORE TOGETHER.

RIGHT NOW, ALL I WANNA DO IS DANCE!!

HERE ARE SOME
RELATIONSHIP
BASICS

QUEER AND TRANS RELATIONSHIPS WILL HAVE THEIR OWN UNIQUE CHALLENGES AND JOYS, BUT THIS SHOULD COVER THE VERY BASICS OF ALL GOOD RELATIONSHIPS

A GOOD PLACE TO START, AS FAR AS RELATIONSHIPS GO, IS WITH SELF-LOVE.

RESPECT YOUR BODY!

KEEP YOURSELF CLEAN, WELL-RESTED, AND WELL-FED AS BEST YOU CAN.

EAT HEALTHY FOODS, GET ENOUGH SLEEP, GET SOME EXERCISE!

A COMFORTABLE BODY CAN GIVE YOU MORE ENERGY TO FEEL THOSE GOOD, CONFIDENT FEELINGS.

IF YOU STRUGGLE WITH SELF-HARM OR SUBSTANCE ABUSE, KNOW THAT YOU'RE NOT ALONE, AND THERE ARE RESOURCES AT THE END OF THE BOOK TO HELP OUT.

DATE YOURSELF FIRST!

IT'S IMPORTANT TO KNOW HOW TO BE COMFORTABLE BY YOURSELF.

GETTING USED TO ENJOYING YOUR OWN COMPANY IS A GOOD WAY TO GET TO KNOW YOURSELF AND BUILD YOUR SELF-ESTEEM.

THAT WAY, YOU KNOW THAT YOU ARE A CAPABLE, INTERESTING, FULFILLED PERSON ON YOUR OWN, AND DON'T NEED A PARTNER TO COMPLETE YOU!

PEOPLE ARE NOT TWO HALVES OF ONE WHOLE—THEY'RE TWO WHOLE PEOPLE WHO HOPEFULLY MAKE EACH OTHER'S LIVES BETTER.

SPREAD THE LOVE!

SPEND SOME TIME HELPING OTHERS AND YOU'LL PROBABLY FEEL VERY VALUABLE AND APPRECIATED.

NOTHING BOOSTS CONFIDENCE LIKE DOING A LITTLE GOOD.

WHO KNOWS? YOU MIGHT MEET SOMEBODY CUTE WHO YOU HAVE THINGS IN COMMON WITH WHILE DOING IT.

...EVEN IF YOU HAVE SOME ROADBLOCKS IN YOUR DAILY LIFE THAT CAN SLOW YOU DOWN LIKE MONEY, FAMILY PROBLEMS, OR GRIEF.

A LITTLE SPARK OF SELF-LOVE CAN MAKE A WORLD OF DIFFERENCE—NOT JUST IN THE CONTEXT OF RELATIONSHIPS.

THE ODDS ARE THAT THE PERSON YOU HAVE A CRUSH ON IN HIGH SCHOOL WON'T WIND UP BEING YOUR SOULMATE.
I WON'T SAY IT'S IMPOSSIBLE, BUT DEFINITELY UNLIKELY.

BETTER TO LET RELATIONSHIPS DEVELOP NATURALLY AS YOU MEET AND SPEND TIME WITH PEOPLE WHO HAVE THINGS IN COMMON WITH YOU.

FORCING A RELATIONSHIP TO DEVELOP WITH SOMEBODY YOU MAY NOT BE COMPATIBLE WITH CAN GET MESSY.

TAKE A FEW STEPS BACK FIRST AND SEE WHAT COULD SLIP YOU UP.

IF YOU RUSH INTO RELATIONSHIPS, YOU MIGHT FIND YOURSELF GETTING INVOLVED WITH SOMEBODY YOU COULD REGRET.
HOT!
WOW!
OOH!
SNIP
SNIP
SNAP
NOT EVERYBODY IS THE WAY THEY SEEM AT FIRST GLANCE. ACTING ON ROMANTIC IMPULSES TOO QUICKLY CAN PUT YOU IN SOME DANGEROUS SITUATIONS.
SNAP
SNIP
SNIP
SNIP
SNAP
IT'S NOT A VERY GOOD IDEA TO GO ON DATES WITH PEOPLE YOU DON'T REALLY KNOW OR TRUST YET.
IT'S ALSO IMPORTANT TO KNOW HOW TO RECOGNIZE 'RED FLAGS' AND WARNING SIGNS.

HERE ARE SOME TIPS TO HELP YOU RECOGNIZE SOME NASTY POISONOUS TRAITS:

IT'S GENERALLY A BAD SIGN IF YOUR PARTNER ACTS JEALOUS WHENEVER YOU HANG OUT WITH OTHER FRIENDS OR FAMILY.
YOUR PARTNER ISN'T SUPPOSED TO BE THE MAIN FOCUS OF YOUR LIFE AND THERE IS NO REASON FOR THEM TO EXPECT YOU TO GIVE YOUR ATTENTION TO THEM AND THEM ALONE.
A GOOD PARTNER WOULD SHOW INTEREST IN YOUR FRIENDS AND HOBBIES RATHER THAN TRYING TO CHANGE THEM OR ISOLATE YOU.
AN ABUSIVE PARTNER WILL OFTEN TRY TO GAIN CONTROL OF AS MANY ASPECTS OF YOUR LIFE AS POSSIBLE.
DO NOT LET A PARTNER DICTATE HOW YOU DRESS, WHO YOU ASSOCIATE WITH, OR HOW YOU EXPRESS YOURSELF (UNLESS YOUR OWN BEHAVIOR IS CLEARLY HARMFUL TO OTHERS).
A PARTNER IS THERE TO SUPPORT YOU, NOT CONTROL YOU.
IT'S CAUSE TO BE WARY IF SOMEBODY ASKS YOU TO BE FULLY COMMITTED TO THEM OR PROPOSES MARRIAGE EARLY ON IN A RELATIONSHIP (WITHIN THE FIRST FEW MONTHS).
THIS IS OFTEN A TACTIC TO 'CLAIM' A PARTNER AND THUS GAIN CONTROL OF THEM.

A 'GASLIGHTING' PARTNER WILL ALWAYS BE TWISTING THE TRUTH.
THIS PARTNER WILL TRY TO DISTORT YOUR EXPERIENCES AND RE-WRITE YOUR MEMORIES.
IF YOU CLEARLY REMEMBER THE WAY SOMETHING HAPPENED AND YOUR PARTNER TRIES TO CONVINCE YOU OTHERWISE, OR IF THEY OFTEN DRAMATICALLY PLAY THE VICTIM IN AN ARGUMENT— IT'S LIKELY THAT YOU'RE BEING GASLIGHTED.
YOUR PARTNER SHOULD NOT BE KEEPING BASIC DETAILS ABOUT THEIR LIFE A SECRET FROM YOU.
THEY ALSO SHOULD NOT BE ASHAMED OF HAVING YOU FOR A PARTNER OR TELLING FRIENDS/PEERS/FAMILY ABOUT YOU.
THIS DOES NOT SHOW TRUST OR AFFECTION, AND BEHAVIOR LIKE THIS SHOULD BE TREATED WITH CAUTION.
SHHHH!
FOLKS WHO BEHAVE IN THESE TOXIC WAYS CAN EXIST IN ANY COMMUNITY OF PEOPLE. DON'T THINK THAT 'PEOPLE LIKE YOU' WOULDN'T BEHAVE THIS WAY.
IT'S A GOOD IDEA TO MONITOR YOURSELF AS WELL, IN CASE YOU EVER START TO SHOW ANY OF THOSE NASTY TRAITS TOO.
SET AN EXAMPLE FOR HOW YOU WOULD LIKE OTHERS TO TREAT YOU.

A GOOD RELATIONSHIP OFTEN FEELS LIKE A FRIENDSHIP BUT A BIT DEEPER.
IT'S BUILT ON TRUST, RESPECT, AND PERSONALITY (AS WELL AS AESTHETICS IN MANY WAYS).
IF YOU GENUINELY CARE FOR AND RESPECT ONE ANOTHER, TALKING TO YOUR PARTNER SHOULD NEVER FEEL DAUNTING OR UNSAFE.
LOVE IS LESS ABOUT 'FINDING SOMEBODY,' AND MORE ABOUT DEVELOPING RELATIONSHIPS.
TAKING A FRIENDSHIP OR CRUSH TO THE NEXT LEVEL, MAYBE?

IT'S ALSO A-OK TO GET REJECTED! EVERYBODY DOES, NO MATTER WHO THEY ARE.
ATTRACTIVENESS AND AESTHETICS ARE ALL RELATIVE AND SO MANY DIFFERENT CIRCUMSTANCES CAN CAUSE A REJECTION. DON'T SWEAT THE SMALL STUFF AND MOVE ON AT THE PACE YOU NEED TO!
AS LONG AS YOU AND YOUR CRUSH UNDERSTAND EACH OTHER AND TALK THINGS OUT, ANY AWKWARDNESS FROM THE REJECTION SORT OF FADES AWAY AFTER A WHILE (IN MOST CASES).

BREAKUPS ALSO SOMETIMES NEED TO HAPPEN—
WHETHER THEY'RE FOREVER OR FOR A WEEK.
IT'S OK TO TAKE SPACE AWAY FROM SOMEBODY IF YOU NEED IT, AND VICE VERSA.
IT'S ALSO EQUALLY FINE TO NOT BE FRIENDS AND NEVER TALK AGAIN!
IT ALL DEPENDS ON THE KIND OF RELATIONSHIP, LIKE MOST THINGS DO.
BREAKUPS CAN ALSO ALLOW FORMER PARTNERS TO BUILD AMAZING FRIENDSHIPS.
EXES CAN BECOME GREAT AND TRUSTWORTHY FRIENDS...
IF THINGS ENDED ON THE RIGHT TERMS.
THERE'S ALSO NOTHING WRONG WITH GETTING BACK TOGETHER LATER ON, AS LONG AS EVERYBODY UNDERSTANDS THE SITUATION AND CONSENTS, TOTALLY.
STALKING SOMEBODY TO GET THEM BACK WOULD BE AN EXAMPLE OF WHAT NOT TO DO.

FINALLY, THE MOST INTEGRAL PART OF A HEALTHY, HAPPY, AND FUNCTIONAL RELATIONSHIPS IS
GOOD COMMUNICATION
THIS ESPECIALLY APPLIES WHEN ARGUMENTS INEVITABLY POP UP.

IT'S A MYTH THAT GOOD PARTNERS SHOULDN'T FIGHT. DISAGREEMENT IS ALL A PART OF ASSERTING ONE'S OWN PERSONALITY IN A RELATIONSHIP.
THE ISSUE IS WHEN DISAGREEMENT TURNS AGGRESSIVE OR TOXIC.

WHILE DISAGREEING IS INEVITABLE, KEEPING IT FROM BLOSSOMING INTO A BIG STINKY FIGHT TAKES A LITTLE FINESSE.

MAKE SURE YOU START FROM A CLEAR AND CALM MINDSET.
IF YOU AREN'T FEELING CALM, IT MIGHT BE A GOOD IDEA TO TAKE SOME SPACE AND HAVE A LITTLE 'TIME OUT' BEFORE STARTING A DISCUSSION.
ALSO, BE SURE TO COME FROM A PLACE OF RESPECT.
YOUR PARTNER SHOULD BE YOUR ALLY, NOT YOUR ENEMY.
IF THE LATTER IS TRUE, IT MIGHT BE TIME TO RE-EVALUATE YOUR RELATIONSHIP.
IN ORDER FOR A CONFLICT TO BE RESOLVED NEATLY, BOTH PARTIES MUST BE SOLUTION-ORIENTED.
THERE IS NO POINT TRYING TO SOLVE A PROBLEM THAT YOU DON'T WANT SOLVED IN THE FIRST PLACE.
FOCUSING ON 'WINNING' A FIGHT WILL ONLY BRING TROUBLE, AND RESENTMENT IS ROTTEN.
TRY YOUR BEST TO LET THE LITTLE THINGS GO.
NAME-CALLING, PERSONAL JABS, AND PHYSICAL VIOLENCE ARE DIRTY TACTICS. DON'T STOOP TO THEM.

AFTERCARE IS VERY IMPORTANT, TOO. MAKE SURE THAT BOTH OF YOU END ON GOOD TERMS (IF POSSIBLE).
MAKE IT CLEAR THAT YOU STILL CARE FOR ONE ANOTHER.
SUCCESSFUL DISCUSSIONS ARE BEST LEFT WITHOUT CLIFFHANGERS.
PHONES ONLY FUNCTION WHEN BOTH RECEIVERS ARE WORKING. SIMILARLY, COMMUNICATION DOESN'T WORK UNLESS BOTH PEOPLE HEAR WHAT THE OTHER HAS TO SAY.
IF YOU KEEP THAT IN MIND, YOUR ROMANTIC RELATIONSHIPS MIGHT JUST GO A BIT MORE SMOOTHLY... AS MAY YOUR FRIENDSHIPS.
C

EVERY DAY, I GROW CLOSER TO YOU.

AT FIRST THIS WAS GOOD THING.

BUT NOW, IT'S HARDER TO TAKE TIME FOR OURSELVES. FOR OUR FRIENDS.

I THOUGHT IN ORDER TO FEEL WHOLE WE NEEDED TO BE TOGETHER, ALWAYS.

BUT I REALIZE NOW THIS ISN'T GOOD FOR US.
I LOVE YOU. BUT WE NEED SPACE TO GROW TOGETHER AGAIN.

I'VE BEEN THINKING THE SAME. IT'S TIME WE STOP GROWING INTO EACH OTHER AND BLOOM ALONGSIDE ONE ANOTHER.

OUTRO

IMAGINE A BIG QUILT MADE OF COLORFUL PATCHES, PATTERNS, AND SHAPES STITCHED TOGETHER. THIS IS HOW I SEE THE QUEER COMMUNITY: MADE UP OF UNIQUE STORIES, EXPERIENCES, AND IDEAS. AS OUR UNDERSTANDING OF DIFFERENT IDENTITIES GROW, WE MUST REMEMBER THAT NOT EVERYONE CAN SHARE AND FIT UNDER THE QUILT UNLESS WE INVITE THEM IN, OR MAKE THE QUILT BIGGER.

QUEER AND TRANSGENDER PEOPLE HAVE LONG BEEN PERCEIVED AS A SMALL, HIDDEN MINORITY. THERE ARE WAY MORE OF US THAN IT LOOKS LIKE. TRUST ME, WE'RE PRETTY DARN GOOD AT FINDING EACH OTHER. WHILE WE DIDN'T HAVE THE LANGUAGE AVAILABLE TO US WHEN WE WERE YOUNGER, A NUMBER OF MY CLOSEST CHILDHOOD FRIENDS AND I NOW IDENTIFY AS QUEER OR TRANS. I THINK IT'S AMAZING THAT WE GRAVITATED TO ONE ANOTHER WHILE STILL UNSURE OF WHO WE WERE. HOWEVER, A BOOK LIKE THIS COULD HAVE REALLY HELPED US ALL OUT.

TO THE READER WHO PICKED THIS BOOK UP TO LEARN AND REFLECT UPON YOUR OWN IDENTITY: WE HOPE THAT WE'VE BEEN ABLE TO PROVIDE YOU WITH NEW KNOWLEDGE ABOUT THE RANGE OF EXPERIENCES LGBTQ+ PEOPLE CAN HAVE! IF YOU ALREADY KNEW MOST OF THIS STUFF, THAT'S AWESOME! THIS COULD BE A REALLY GREAT OPPORTUNITY TO PASS THE BOOK ON TO SOMEONE IN YOUR LIFE WHO YOU'D LIKE TO START A DIALOGUE WITH.

TO THE CURIOUS FAMILY MEMBER OR FRIEND OF SOMEONE WHO IDENTIFIES AS LGBTQ+: THANK YOU SO MUCH FOR PICKING UP THIS BOOK. LET THIS BE A JUMPING OFF POINT FOR FURTHER LEARNING AND CONVERSATION. WHILE THIS CAN ACT AS A USEFUL TOOL KIT TO HELP YOU BE A SUPPORTIVE ALLY, REMEMBER THAT LANGUAGE IS ALWAYS EVOLVING, AND SO ARE YOUR LOVED ONES. BE PATIENT WITH THEM, AS WELL AS YOURSELVES. WE'RE ALL HUMAN, AND MISTAKES HAPPEN! IF YOU USE THE WRONG PRONOUNS FOR SOMEONE, IT IS OKAY TO APOLOGIZE AND MOVE ON. (SEE *A QUICK & EASY GUIDE FOR THEY/THEM PRONOUNS* FOR A MORE IN-DEPTH DISCUSSION ON THIS!) JUST BE READY TO LEARN, UNLEARN, AND LEARN SOME MORE.

AND LASTLY, TO THOSE WHO PICKED THIS BOOK UP BECAUSE YOU ARE QUESTIONING: THIS VERY WELL COULD BE YOUR EARLY STEPS IN YOUR IDENTITY VOYAGE! WE'RE REALLY EXCITED FOR YOU. BUT REMEMBER, THERE IS NO NEED TO RUSH. IT'S OKAY TO EXPLORE YOUR IDENTITY AT THE PACE THAT FEELS MOST NATURAL FOR YOU.

WHEN I STARTED TO DEVELOP THE WORLD OF THE SPROUTLINGS, I THOUGHT ABOUT A KINDER WORLD WITHOUT OPPRESSIVE, ARCHAIC GENDER EXPECTATIONS. WHILE THIS MAY SEEM LIKE AN IDYLLIC VISION, I REALIZED THAT EVEN IN A WORLD WHERE A SPECTRUM OF IDENTITIES IS VISIBLE AND WELCOMED, THERE'S STILL A LOT TO NAVIGATE INTERNALLY AND INTERPERSONALLY. IT IS MY HOPE THAT THE SPROUTLINGS CAN ACT LIKE TINY GUIDES TO ANYONE GRAPPLING WITH BIG QUESTIONS OF HOW TO BE AND HOW TO LOVE.

HERE'S TO BUILDING A UNITED, SAFE, AND WARM COMMUNITY TOGETHER. THERE'S PLENTY OF ROOM FOR ALL!

~J.K. ZUCKERBERG

DESIGN A PAIR OF
FRIENDSHIP
JACKETS!

CREATE PATCH DESIGNS, DRAW ON PINS, AND ADD EMBROIDERY!
THESE DESIGNS CAN TAKE A STANCE ON SOMETHING YOU CARE ABOUT, SPREAD SOME AWARENESS, OR JUST BE FUN AND EXPRESSIVE!
DESIGN THEM YOURSELF, WITH A PAL, SIBLING, OR ANYONE ELSE!

DEAR PAST
OR FUTURE SELF:

CREATE YOUR OWN
SPROUT-SONA!
IF YOU WERE A SPROUTLING, WHAT WOULD YOU LOOK LIKE? THERE'S PLENTY OF ROOM TO BE INVENTIVE AS YOU DESIGN YOUR SPROUTLING SELF. WE CAN'T WAIT TO SEE THEM!
ADD SOME PLANTS YOU LIKE, OR MAKE LEAVES & FOLIAGE OUT OF SHAPES YOU ENJOY!
THINK OF SOME CRITTERS YOU LIKE. TRY MIXING 'EM TOGETHER!
YOUR AUTHORS HAD A BLAST DESIGNING THEIR OWN:

INTRODUCING:

HOW TO MAKE A MINI ZINE!!

LET'S START OUT BY GATHERING MATERIALS! YOU WILL NEED:

NOW FIND A FLAT WORKSPACE TO FOLD YOUR ZINE ON:

IF YOU WANT TO SHARE YOUR ZINE WITH THE WORLD, THE NEXT STEP IS DISTRIBUTION! GO TO YOUR LOCAL PRINT CENTER OR LIBRARY, MAKE SOME COPIES, AND YOU'RE READY TO GO! YOU CAN TAKE YOUR ZINES TO SMALL PRESS FAIRS, LOCAL COMIC SHOPS, OR JUST CARRY THEM IN YOUR BAG TO HAND OUT WHEREVER! YOU CAN ALSO SCAN AND PUBLISH YOUR ZINE ONLINE (JUST BE SURE TO CREDIT YOURSELF AND BE RESPECTFUL IF YOU'RE SHARING A STORY THAT INVOLVES FRIENDS OR ANYONE OTHER THAN YOURSELF).

HAVE FUN!

MORE RESOURCES!

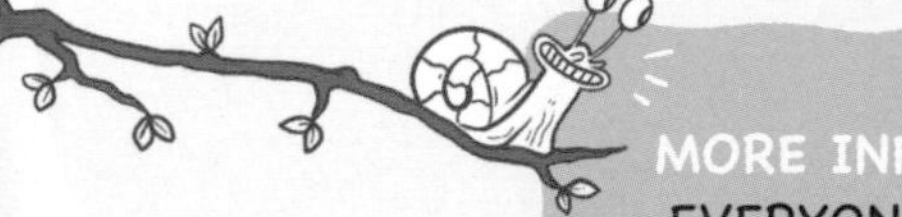

MORE INFORMATION:
EVERYONEISGAY.COM
THETREVORPROJECT.ORG
GLAAD.ORG
HRC.ORG

RELATIONSHIPS AND SEX:
SCARLETEEN.COM

LGBTQ+ YOUTH AND STUDENTS:
GSANETWORK.ORG
GLSEN.ORG
TRUECOLORSFUND.ORG
TRANSSTUDENT.ORG

LGBTQ+ ELDERS:
LGBTAGINGCENTER.ORG
SAGEUSA.ORG

FAMILY MEMBERS, EDUCATORS, AND ALLIES:
PFLAG.ORG
MYKIDISGAY.COM

HOTLINES:
TRANSLIFELINE.ORG
THETREVORPROJECT.ORG
SUICIDEPREVENTIONLIFELINE.ORG
GLBTHOTLINE.ORG

CHECK OUT YOUR LOCAL LIBRARY FOR MORE BOOKS TO READ! MEETUP GROUPS (EITHER IN PERSON OR ONLINE) CAN ALSO BE GREAT PLACES TO FIND RESOURCES AND COMMUNITY.

MADY G.

IS A CARTOONIST AND ILLUSTRATOR BASED IN NEW YORK STATE. NO STRANGER TO WILDLIFE AND NATURAL WONDERS, THEY SPENT MOST OF THEIR CHILDHOOD EXPLORING IN THE NORTHEASTERN U.S. AND IN SOUTHWESTERN CANADA, SURROUNDED BY ALL KINDS OF FLORA AND FAUNA. THEY ARE PASSIONATE ABOUT LGBTQ+ AND HUMAN RIGHTS, ESPECIALLY THE RIGHTS OF TRANSGENDER AND GENDER NON-CONFORMING PEOPLE, AND HOPE TO CONTRIBUTE TO A MORE LOVING AND LESS JUDGEMENTAL WORLD.

J.R. ZUCKERBERG

IS A CARTOONIST, ILLUSTRATOR, AND CRAFTSPERSON LIVING IN BROOKLYN, NY. THEY GREW UP IN THE MIDDLE OF THE WOODS OF NEW YORK STATE AND HAVE ALWAYS DRAWN INSPIRATION FROM THEIR OBSERVATIONS OF FLORA AND FAUNA. THEY'VE CREATED PLAYFUL ILLUSTRATIONS FOR CHILDREN'S MAGAZINES, JOURNAL COMICS GALORE, AND A NUMBER OF SELF-PUBLISHED MINI COMICS. J.R. IS SO EXCITED TO DEBUT THE MICROCOSM OF THE SPROUTLINGS IN *A QUICK & EASY GUIDE TO QUEER & TRANS IDENTITIES*!

ALSO AVAILABLE:

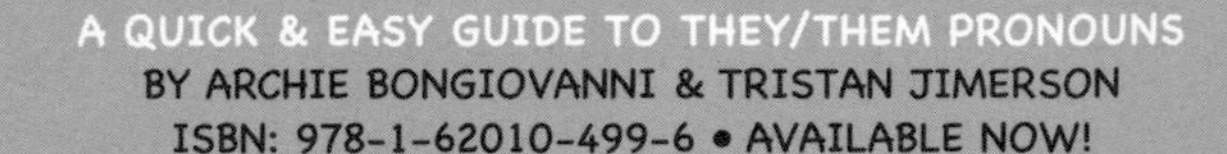